When Mama
Comes Home Tonight

When Mama Comes Home Tonight

BY Eileen Spinelli

ILLUSTRATED BY Jane Dyer

SIMON & SCHUSTER BOOKS FOR YOUNG READERS

Special thanks to Lynn and Willie
—J. D.

SIMON & SCHUSTER BOOKS FOR YOUNG READERS
An imprint of Simon & Schuster Children's Publishing Division
1230 Avenue of the Americas, New York, New York 10020
Text copyright © 1998 by Eileen Spinelli. Illustrations copyright
© 1998 by Jane Dyer. All rights reserved including the right of
reproduction in whole or in part in any form. SIMON & SCHUSTER
BOOKS FOR YOUNG READERS is a trademark of Simon & Schuster.
Book design by Paul Zakris. The text for this book is set in 30-
point Venetian. The illustrations are rendered on Waterford 140
lb. hot press paper with Winsor & Newton watercolors and Caran
D'Ache colored pencils.

Printed and bound in the United States of America

First Edition

10 9 8 7 6 5 4 3 2

LIBRARY OF CONGRESS CATALOGING-IN-PUBLICATION DATA
When Mama comes home tonight / written by Eileen Spinelli;
illustrated by Jane Dyer.

p. cm.

Summary: When Mama arrives home, she and her child enjoy a
series of activities together before bedtime.

ISBN 0-689-81065-2

1. Mother and child—Fiction. 2. Bedtime—Fiction.

3. Stories in rhyme.

I. Dyer, Jane, ill.

PZ8.3.S759 Wh 1998

[E]—dc21

96-53141

To Joan McIntyre and the staff and
friends of Phoenixville Library
—E. S.

For all mothers who come home tired at the end
of the day—wishing you dances down the hall
—J. D.

When Mama comes home from work, dear child,
when Mama comes home tonight,
she'll cover you with kisses,
she'll hug you sweet and tight.

She'll feed you soup and applesauce,
she'll dance you down the hall,

she'll play a game of pat-a-cake,
she'll wrap you in her shawl.

She'll hold you at the window,

she'll help you count the cars.

She'll make three wishes in your name
and tell them to the stars.

When Mama comes home from work, dear child,
when Mama comes home tonight,
she'll say, "Let's put your blocks away—
the red, the green, the white."

She'll fix herself a cup of tea
and let you have a sip.

She'll mend your blue pajamas

and her own pink satin slip.

She'll bathe you soft and gentle,
she'll brush your curly hair,

she'll read your favorite story
in the cozy rocking chair.

She'll find your tattered Teddy

and your fuzzy little sheep.

She'll hush you down with lullabies
until you're near asleep.

She'll tuck you snug beneath the quilt
and leave on one small light,

when Mama comes home from work, dear child,
when Mama comes home tonight.